A Tale of Two Bunnies

By Dion A Shaw Jr

ISBN: 978-0-578-95755-5

Published in the United States.

Once upon a time, there were two bunnies living in a burrow together, Benjamin and Bradley.

Benjamin was a very fit and active bunny rabbit, he loved nothing more than hopping through the fields with his friends.

However, Bradley was a very lazy bunny rabbit and spent most of his time playing video games in the burrow.

SCHOOL

Benjamin tried so hard to convince Bradley to come out and play but his lazy bunny friend refused to budge from the sofa.

“Bradley, Bradley, Bradley! A few of the other bunnies and I are heading out on a run, do you want to come and join in?” Benjamin asked one morning.

“No thank you, I want to finish this game...” Bradley replied without taking his eyes off the screen.

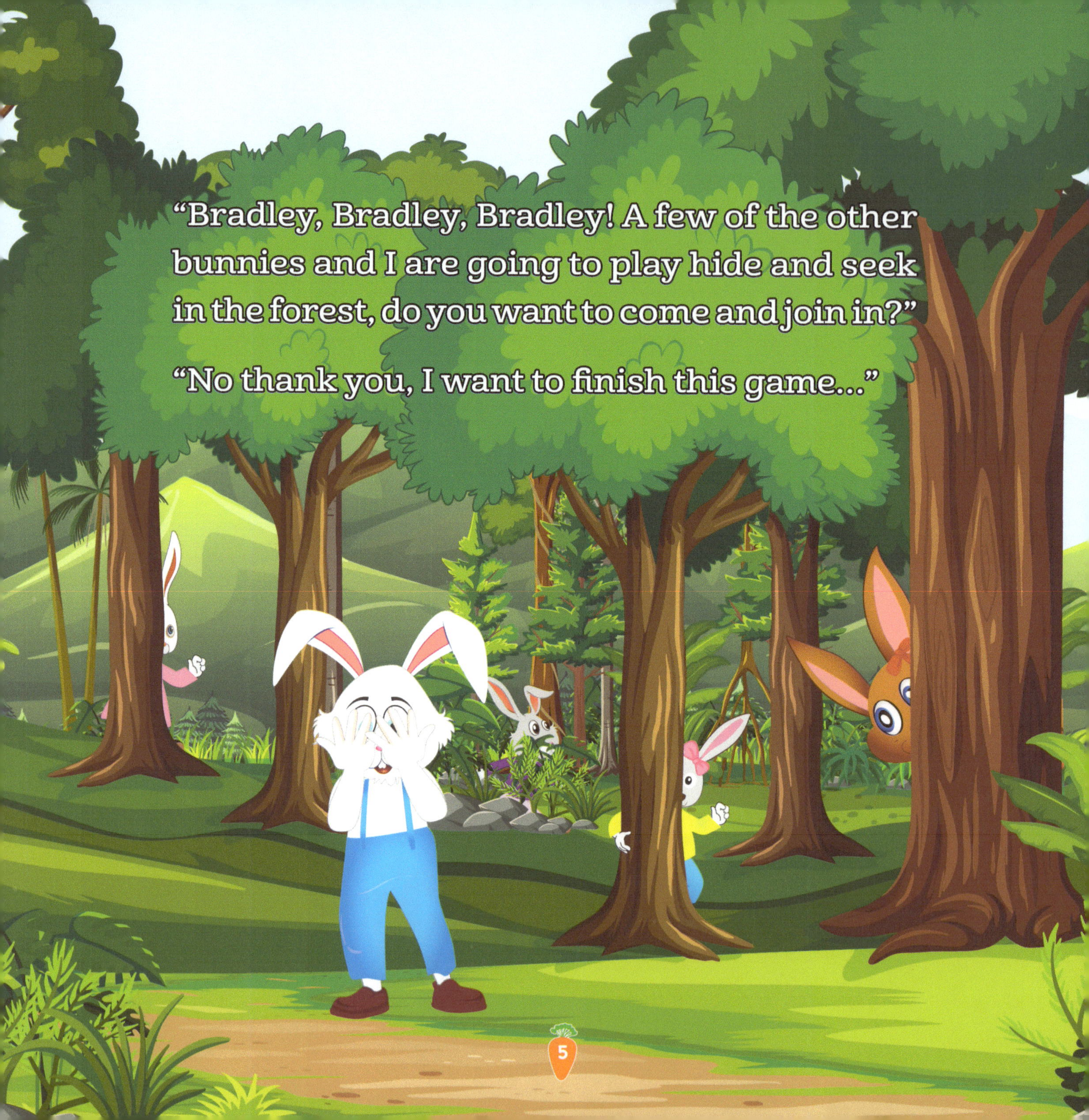

"Bradley, Bradley, Bradley! A few of the other bunnies and I are going to play hide and seek in the forest, do you want to come and join in?"

"No thank you, I want to finish this game..."

"Bradley, Bradley, Bradley! A few of the other bunnies and I are going to play Soccer in the fields, do you want to come and join in?"

"No thank you, I want to finish this game..."

"Bradley, Bradley, Bradley! A few of the other bunnies and I are going to work out in the gym, do you want to come and join in?"

"No thank you, I want to finish this game..."

"Bradley, Bradley, Bradley! A few of the other bunnies and I are going to help the community by painting the new school, do you want to come and join in?"

"No thank you, I want to finish this game..."

SCHOOL

No matter how hard Benjamin tried, he just couldn't get Bradley to move!

He even made up that he had spotted a UFO outside the burrow, but even that didn't get Bradley to take his eyes off the screen.

There was only one thing for it, Benjamin was going to have to hatch a plan!

He and the other bunny rabbits were worried that Bradley was not getting enough exercise and social time. It was important to keep healthy and active, as well as looking after your mental health by laughing with your friends.

Sitting on the sofa, eating junk food and staring at a screen all day was bad for Bradley's body, his mind and his eyes.

Something had to change!

One morning, Benjamin woke up extra early and snuck into the living room to replace the batteries in Bradley's games console with dead ones.

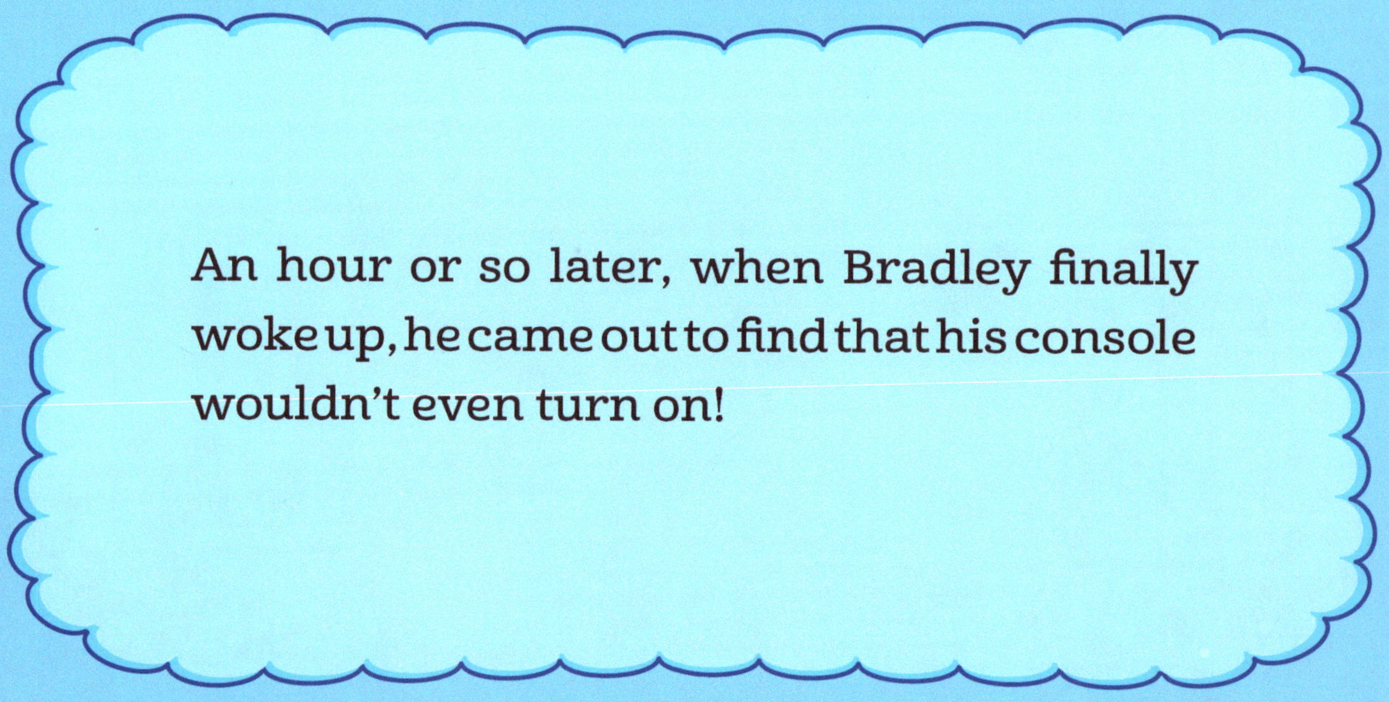

An hour or so later, when Bradley finally woke up, he came out to find that his console wouldn't even turn on!

“Benjamin, Benjamin, Benjamin! We need to go out and get some new batteries for my games console! Where can I get some?” Bradley cried.

“Oh no!” Benjamin exclaimed with a cheeky grin. “Why don’t we go out and see if any of our friends know where to get some.”

Benjamin and Bradley hopped straight out the burrow door in their quest to find batteries and the first stop on their route was Bonnie bunny’s house.

“Hey guys!” she smiled. “It’s great to see you out and about, Bradley. It’s been a while. How can I help?”

“I’m looking for some batteries for my games console, do you have any please?” Bradley begged.

“How many do you need?” Bonnie asked.

"Four," Bradley replied hopefully.

"I'm afraid that I only have one to spare," Bonnie shrugged. "I'll happily let you have it if you guys have time to play a game of tennis with me?"

Bradley wanted that battery more than anything and he was willing to play a quick game of tennis if it meant getting one step closer to his video games.

Bradley, Benjamin, Bonnie and her sister Bettie played tennis for the next hour. It was so much fun! They couldn't stop laughing with Benjamin tripped over his own feet going for a shot.

What surprised Bonnie was that Bradley was actually very good at tennis. Why didn't he do this more often?

Once the game was done, Bradley, Bonnie and Benjamin hopped along to Bobby's house.

"Hey, guys!" Bobby smiled. "I haven't seen you in ages, Bradley!"

"Hi Bobby," Bradley said. "I'm looking for some batteries for my games console, do you have any please?"

"I'm afraid that I only have one to spare," Bobby revealed. "I'll happily let you have it if you can help me to finish painting the new school."

Bradley knew that it was one step closer to getting back to his video games so he agreed to the plan and picked up a can of blue paint.

The four bunnies had so much fun painting the school, especially when Bonnie accidentally lent on the wall and covered her fur in blue! Bradley couldn't stop laughing.

Once it was all done, Bradley, Benjamin, Bonnie and Bobby hopped along to Beth's house.

Like the others, Beth had just the one battery to spare!

"I will happily let you have it if you come and keep me company at the gym," Beth smiled.

So the five bunnies headed straight to the gym and enjoyed a great work out. Bradley used muscles he had forgotten he even had! But he felt much better for it come the end of the session.

GYM

Finally, Bradley, Benjamin, Bonnie, Bobby and Beth hopped over to Bella's house in search of the final battery.

As luck would have it, she had one to spare! However, she wanted the others to play a Soccer match with her in exchange.

It was Bradley, Benjamin, Bonnie vs Beth, Bella and Bobby!

They had so much fun and Bradley was amazing at Soccer.

Once the match ended, Bradley had just one thing to say...

"Shall we play another?"

Benjamin's plan had worked. Bradley was actually having fun away from his video games. If only he knew that there had been spare batteries back at home this entire time...

www.ingramcontent.com/pod-product-compliance
Lightning Source LLC
LaVergne TN
LVHW070203110826
845147LV00002B/482

* 9 7 8 0 5 7 8 9 5 7 5 5 5 *